FOOTBALL FACTOR
SAFE KEEPING

First published in 2013 by Wayland

Text copyright © Alan Durant 2013
Illustrations © Wayland 2013

Wayland
338 Euston Road
London NW1 3BH

Wayland Australia
Level 17/207 Kent Street
Sydney, NSW 2000

Series Editor: Victoria Brooker
Series design: Robert Walster and Basement68
Cover design: Lisa Peacock
Consultant: Dee Reid

A CIP catalogue record for this book is available
from the British Library.
Dewey number: 823.9'2-dc23

ISBN 978 0 7502 7984 0

2 4 6 8 10 9 7 5 3 1

Printed in China

Wayland is a division of Hachette Children's Books,
an Hachette UK Company
www.hachette.co.uk

Freestylers

FOOTBALL FACTOR
SAFE KEEPING

Alan Durant and Andrew Chiu

WAYLAND
www.waylandbooks.co.uk

"Where's my lucky horsehoe?" said Tom.

Tom was Sheldon's keeper.

He had a horseshoe on a chain.

He said it brought him good luck.

Every match Tom took the
horseshoe on the pitch.
It was in his cap for safe keeping.
He put the cap at the back of the goal.

But today the horseshoe was missing.

What a day to lose it!

Sheldon were playing the Cup semi-final!

Tom was in a panic.

He searched in his kit bag.

He looked around the changing room.

But he could not find his lucky horseshoe.

Sheldon were playing Denley Athletic.

Tom didn't make a very good start.

He dropped a cross …

but Ledley cleared the ball.

A shot went through his legs …
but hit the post.

He miskicked a back pass.

It went to the Athletic striker, Eeshan.

Eeshan shot first time…
but the ball hit the bar.
Maybe Tom was in luck after all!

11

But then disaster struck.

The Athletic striker shot again.

Tom dived full length.

He pushed the ball against the post.

But the ball bounced back.
It hit Tom on the back…
and rolled over the line.

13

"Goal!"

The Denley Athletic players
jumped for joy.

Tom couldn't believe it.

"Bad luck," said Ledley.

It wasn't bad luck, thought Tom.
It was terrible. He had to find his
lucky horseshoe.

At half-time Tom looked
in the changing room again.
Joe Ford, Sheldon's coach, stopped him.

"Forget about that horseshoe," he said.
"Good keepers make their own luck.
Trust in your skill."

Sheldon were better after the interval.
They kept the ball in Denley's half.
Tom just looked on as Sheldon attacked.

Robbie played a one-two with Naz.
Then he smashed the ball in the net.
Sheldon were level!

There were five minutes left.

Tom kicked the ball up field.

Kyle headed on to Zoltan.

Zoltan passed to Danny.

Danny sprinted down the wing
and crossed. Naz leapt and scored!
Tom did a cartwheel.

Denley Athletic made one last attack.

The ref's whistle was in his mouth.

The ball bounced in the penalty area.

Tom rushed to get it…

But he slipped.

He crashed into the Denley striker.

The ref blew his whistle.

It wasn't the end of the match.

It was a penalty!

Tom cursed his luck.

If only he hadn't lost his horseshoe.

Then he remembered what Joe had said.

The Denley striker ran up to the spot.
He kicked the ball.

Tom dived right.

He tipped the ball against the post.

It bounced back…

safely into his arms!

Sheldon had won.

They were in the final!

Tom danced off the pitch.

Joe Ford met him.

He had a smile on his face.

"Look what I found inside your spare boots," he said.

"I don't need that anymore,"
Tom laughed. "Good keepers make
their own luck!"

Read more stories about Sheldon Rovers.

Sheldon Rovers have made it to the Cup final. It is their manager Dave Brown's last match. Will Danny, Robby, Naz, Ledley and Tom play their best? Can they make Dave's day and win the Cup?

Danny is playing his first match for Sheldon Rovers. It is the first round of the Cup. He needs to play well to keep his place. But will nerves get the better of him?

Naz is Sheldon Rover's top scorer. He is a goal machine. But suddenly things start to go wrong. He can't score at all. He loses his place in the team. Will he ever get his goal touch back?

Tom plays in goal for Sheldon Rovers. He has a lucky horseshoe that he takes to every match. But on Cup semi-final day it goes missing. Things start to go wrong. Has Tom's luck run out?

Robby keeps getting sent off. Now he has got a three-match ban and he feels down. Can he learn to control his temper? Will he ever get back in the team?

Ledley is a defender for Sheldon Rovers. He has been out injured for months. His first game is the Cup quarter final. Will he last the game? Will his tackling be strong enough?

FOR TEACHERS

About Freestylers

Freestylers is a series of carefully levelled stories, especially geared for struggling readers of both sexes. With very low reading age and high interest age, these books are humorous, fun, up-to-the-minute and edgy. Core characters provide familiarity in all of the stories, build confidence and ease pupils from one story through to the next, accelerating reading progress.

Freestylers can be used for both guided and independent reading. To make the most of the books you can:

- Focus on making each reading session successful. Talk about the text before the pupil starts reading. Introduce the characters, the storyline and any unfamiliar vocabulary.

- Encourage the pupil to talk about the book during reading and after reading. How would they have felt if they were one of the characters playing for Sheldon Rovers? How would they have dealt with the situations that the players found themselves in?

- Talk about which parts of the story they like best and why.

For guidance, this story has been approximately measured to:

National Curriculum Level: 1B   ATOS: 2.1
Reading Age: 6   Lexile ® Measure [confirmed]: 300L
Book Band: Orange